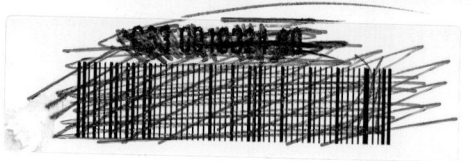

THIS Picture Knight BOOK BELONGS TO

....

For Mimi, with my love

GUMDROP'S
MERRY CHRISTMAS

Story and pictures by Val Biro

Picture Knight

HODDER AND STOUGHTON

IT WAS Christmas Eve. The snow
sparkled on the road and lay thick
on the roof of a small garage.
Had you looked inside, you would
have seen a remarkable car – a blue
car with brass lamps – which you'd
have recognised immediately as an
Austin Clifton Heavy 12/4, vintage
1926 – Gumdrop himself!

Mr Josiah Oldcastle was filling
Gumdrop's radiator with warm water
before driving out to fetch the
Christmas turkey. His dog Horace
could hardly wait: he liked turkey.

Mr Oldcastle had nearly finished when he heard a booming voice at the door: 'HO HO HO!' He nearly dropped the can when he saw who it was.

It was Father Christmas! There he stood, white beard and all, laughing merrily.

'Well, well, you must have thought I was real,' he said. 'Can't you recognise me? It's me! I'm your neighbour Bumblebee pretending to be Father Christmas!'

He explained that it was for the Christmas Party at the Village Hall and that he had come to ask for a lift. 'My sleigh and reindeer are already there,' he added.

'A reindeer?' asked Mr Oldcastle.

'Well, it's really Farmer Hearn's pony in disguise, but the sleigh is real enough. By the way,' he went on, 'you'd better call me Father Christmas for the day, in case I forget who I am, HO HO HO!'

Mr Bumblebee climbed into Gumdrop.
Horace kept barking because he could smell
cat on Mr Bumblebee's clothes and
Horace hated cats.

Mr Oldcastle climbed in too and pressed
the starter button, but nothing happened.
With dismay he realised that the starter,
which had been giving a lot of trouble,
had finally broken down.

'And I don't know if I can get another
one,' he complained as he took out the
starting handle to turn Gumdrop by hand.
It was hard work and Mr Oldcastle was
quite hot and bothered by the time they
managed to drive out at last.

Everybody smiled as Gumdrop came down the street, especially
when they saw Father Christmas sitting in the back. He waved
graciously and wished everyone a Merry Christmas, with a
booming HO HO HO! for good measure.

Mr Oldcastle left Father Christmas at the Village Hall and
promised to come back after tea to take him home.

First, Mr Oldcastle drove to the toyshop. He left the engine running so that he would not have to start Gumdrop by hand again. He asked some children to stand guard in case there were some vintage car thieves about.

Fortunately Gumdrop was still there when he came out,
laden with parcels for his grandchildren. He had even
bought some presents for Gumdrop's guards who were delighted
and thought that Christmas had already arrived!

Then Mr Oldcastle drove out to an old-fashioned garage
which might just have a new starter for Gumdrop. He left
the engine running again and went in. As soon as his back
was turned someone jumped into Gumdrop and, without a
by-your-leave, drove the car right away!

'Stop, thief, stop!' yelled Mr Oldcastle and dashed out
to save his precious car. Gumdrop was gathering speed as
Horace leapt in hot pursuit, with Mr Oldcastle panting along
behind. Just as unexpectedly Gumdrop slowed down and
stopped, and the vintage car thief got out.

'Forgive me,' he grinned, 'but I used to have a car just like yours many years ago, and I could not resist the temptation to drive this beauty. Thank you so much, sir, you've made my Christmas!' He raised his hat and walked away, skipping jauntily.

Mr Oldcastle could not bring himself to be angry with a fellow enthusiast, but he resolved that in future he would always switch off the engine.

The garage did not have a starter motor after all, and Mr Oldcastle wondered if he would ever find one. But now he had to fetch the Christmas turkey. He parked outside the butcher's shop and this time he switched off the engine. He was not going to take any more risks!

When he came out he suddenly realised that he had left the starting handle back at his own garage! So the butcher and his customers gave Gumdrop a hearty push-start and Mr Oldcastle wished them a Merry Christmas as he drove away.

He went to deliver the presents to his grandchildren and
stayed for tea. Afterwards they played games, but all too
soon it was time to go and collect Mr Bumblebee from the
Village Hall.

Halfway there they met him, white beard and all, driving
in his sleigh. Farmer Hearn's pony was so well disguised
that he looked exactly like a reindeer.

'So there you are, Father Christmas,' said Mr Oldcastle
(who had not forgotten what Mr Bumblebee had asked him).
'But tell me, why is your pony limping?'

It appeared that the poor animal had a splinter in his foot and needed a vet. So they decided to park the sleigh and put the pony on the back seat of Gumdrop. Father Christmas brought his sack and sat himself in the front, with Horace on his lap.

The dog didn't seem to mind the smell of cat this time, and even licked Father Christmas on the nose. When all was ready they set out. On the way, people were enchanted to see a reindeer sitting in Gumdrop, along with Father Christmas and a dog. He waved and wished them all a Merry Christmas – without once booming HO HO HO!

The vet said that she would have to give the reindeer an anaesthetic before she could remove the splinter. Then she turned to Mr Oldcastle with a puzzled look. 'But why did you say this was a pony?' she asked.

Before he could explain, Father Christmas said they had better hurry because he still had presents to deliver. They would have to go in Gumdrop and call back later for the reindeer.

It was already getting dark when they set off. Father Christmas gave directions while he started to sort out the parcels in his sack.

'I say, Father Christmas,' chuckled Mr Oldcastle as he drove along, 'you do take your job seriously!'

'Of course I do,' replied Father Christmas solemnly. 'After all, the children expect me to come tonight and I must not disappoint them.'

And Horace licked him on the nose again.

'Stop here,' said Father Christmas
when they reached the village,
and he got out of Gumdrop.

He flung the sack over his shoulder,
marched down the garden path, climbed
up the house, walked across the roof
and dropped a parcel down the chimney.

Mr Oldcastle was utterly appalled to
see this. Bumblebee was *really* overdoing
his part of Father Christmas!

But the same thing happened at the
next house – and the next – until
Father Christmas had finished all his
deliveries.

'Phew!' said Mr Oldcastle when he
got his breath back. 'It's just as well
there weren't any policemen about!'

At least Father Christmas had
done his job silently, without a
single HO HO HO!

When they got back to the vet, the animal was perfectly
well again and wide awake. Father Christmas said that they
had to hurry because he had to collect his sleigh and there
was a very long journey ahead of him and the reindeer.
This time it was Mr Oldcastle who looked puzzled.

Just as they settled into Gumdrop, the engine stalled. Of course there was neither a starter nor a starting handle.

'Never mind,' said Father Christmas, 'we shall give you a pull-and-push start.'

So the reindeer pulled from the front, Father Christmas pushed from behind, and Gumdrop started with the utmost ease.

They found the sleigh where they had left it, and Father
Christmas hitched up the reindeer. When all was ready he
turned to Mr Oldcastle.

'Thank you for all your help,' he said. 'I don't know
where we'd have been without this beautiful vehicle of yours.
Now then, what would *you* like for Christmas?'

'Oh, a new starter for Gumdrop of course,' blurted out Mr
Oldcastle before he could stop himself, though he knew that
it was ridiculous to ask Mr Bumblebee for one.

Father Christmas just smiled, reached into his almost empty sack and pulled out . . . a brand new starter for Gumdrop!

Mr Oldcastle was so amazed he couldn't speak. And before he knew it, he got out his tools and lay flat under Gumdrop to fix the new starter in place. It was a perfect fit.

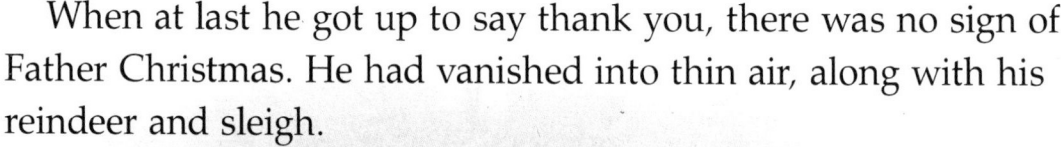

When at last he got up to say thank you, there was no sign of Father Christmas. He had vanished into thin air, along with his reindeer and sleigh.

Mr Oldcastle looked about in a daze, but it began
to snow just then and it was difficult to see.

Suddenly he heard a familiar 'HO HO HO!' and he turned
round. Sure enough, there they were again, coming
through the snowflakes towards him.

But now the reindeer
looked just like Farmer Hearn's
pony in disguise, and Father Christmas,
who had taken off his white beard, now looked
just like Mr Bumblebee! And Horace the dog began
to bark because he could smell cat again!
'Where have you been?' asked Mr Bumblebee. 'I've been
waiting for you at the Village Hall for ages!'

Mr Oldcastle just stood there, marvelling. Here was
Mr Bumblebee with the pony – so could that limping reindeer
have been a REAL reindeer after all? Even more wonderfully,
was the Father Christmas who gave him the starter the REAL
Father Christmas himself? It was a big question, but Horace
looked as though he knew the answer perfectly well.

As if to prove it, Gumdrop's new starter began to whirr and
the engine came to life with a sound that seemed to say
Merry Christmas!

British Library Cataloguing in Publication Data

A catalogue record for this title
is available from the British Library

ISBN 0 340 60051 9

Text and illustrations copyright © Val Biro 1992

The right of Val Biro to be identified as the author of
this work has been asserted by him in accordance with the
Copyright, Designs and Patents Act 1988.

First published 1992
Picture Knight edition first published 1993

Published by Hodder and Stoughton Children's Books,
a division of Hodder and Stoughton Ltd,
Mill Road, Dunton Green, Sevenoaks, Kent TN13 2YA

Printed in Belgium by Proost International Book Production